Pooch Parlour

Passion for Fashion

For Amelia and Erin – KC

To Ben and Kali, who both love pugs – JAD

STRIPES PUBLISHING
An imprint of Little Tiger Press
1 The Coda Centre, 189 Munster Road,
London SW6 6AW

This paperback edition first published
in Great Britain in 2014.

Text copyright © Katy Cannon, 2014
Illustrations copyright © Artful Doodlers, 2014
Cover illustration copyright © Simon Mendez, 2014
Photographic images courtesy of www.shutterstock.com

ISBN: 978-1-84715-442-2

A CIP catalogue record for this book is available
from the British Library.

Printed and bound in the UK.

2 4 6 8 10 9 7 5 3 1

Passion for Fashion

Katy Cannon

stripes

"This," Abi said, pushing open the door with the "All Dogs Welcome" sign on it, "is Pooch Parlour!"

"Wow!" Emily stared through the doorway without moving, which made Abi smile. Emily, Abi's best friend, had arrived in London the night before. She was spending the weekend there, visiting Abi. Emily had already been amazed by Aunt Tiffany's flat, Aunt Tiffany's miniature dachshund, Hugo, and all the different shops near the luxury dog-grooming salon. But it looked like Pooch Parlour itself was the most impressive thing Emily had seen yet!

Abi's bichon frise, Lulu, sneaked through Emily's legs and padded into the parlour, but Emily stayed still.

"You can go in, you know," Abi joked, and Emily grinned at her before stepping through the doorway.

Emily had picked the best possible weekend to visit, Abi thought. Pooch Parlour was buzzing with activity, as everyone prepared to move off-site to the Pawchester Hotel. The very glamorous – but dog-friendly – hotel was holding the Best Friends for Life fashion show that very night! Aunt Tiffany had promised that the girls would get to watch the show, and tomorrow Abi could give Emily a glimpse of what a normal day at Pooch Parlour was like.

"It's incredible," Emily said, as she explored the reception area, staring at the photos on the walls of celebrities and their dogs, and the glass cabinets full of sparkly dog accessories.

"It really is," Abi agreed.

"And you get to work here every day, all summer." Emily sighed. "You're so lucky."

Abi knew that she *was* lucky. Not every nine-year-old girl had an aunt who ran a grooming parlour for the pets of the rich and famous, and not every nine-year-old girl got to spend a whole summer helping out there. It was hard work, taking care of the dogs, and doing whatever the Pooch Parlour staff needed her to do, but Abi loved it. And it was good practice for her future dream career – working with the animals who starred in films and on TV.

"Well, this weekend *you* get to work here

too," Abi said. "Come on, I want to show you around."

At that moment, Hugo scurried under the curtain behind the reception desk, dressed in a bright red T-shirt and a black beret, followed by Aunt Tiffany. Lulu scampered over to Hugo.

"I'm afraid your tour might have to wait, Abi," Aunt Tiffany said. "I have a job for you two, and it means leaving Pooch Parlour for the whole day."

Abi's eyes widened. If they were going to be out for the whole day, that must mean... "You want us to help out at the fashion show?

Really?" She bounced on her toes at the idea. Abi had been thrilled they'd simply get to watch the show. She hadn't imagined they might get to spend the whole day there.

Aunt Tiffany nodded. "That's right. I need you two to shadow Mel — that's our wardrobe assistant, Emily. Abi's already learned so much about grooming and looking after the dogs, I know you'll both be a big help when Mel's getting the dogs in and out of their costumes. We want them all to look adorable for their big moments!"

"I've never dressed a dog in actual clothes before," Emily said anxiously.

"Don't worry," Aunt Tiffany said, with a gentle smile. "Abi will soon teach you, I'm sure."

"Should we go and find Mel now?" Abi asked.

Aunt Tiffany nodded. "I think she's in the wardrobe room, getting the costumes together," she said. "I'll see you both over at the hotel, later. I need to set up the mobile grooming stations for the dog models."

"OK," Abi said. "Come on, Lulu!"

Lulu scampered ahead, leading the way to the wardrobe room, with the girls hurrying along behind. The fluffy little dog knew her way around Pooch Parlour almost as well as Abi did!

"Is Mel nice?" Emily asked, as they approached the wardrobe room.

"She's lovely," Abi reassured her friend. "And the wardrobe room is great. It's like a real shop, but with clothes for dogs. Look!" She pushed open the door. "Oh!"

Instead of the usual neat racks and shelves filled with outfits and accessories, the wardrobe room was in absolute chaos. Jumpers and dresses and T-shirts and hats were everywhere, hanging off chairs and pegs and rails. The carefully ordered drawers of collars and bows, grouped by colour, had all been pulled out and mixed up.

Abi gasped and suddenly, from the middle of the mess, Mel stood up. Her ponytail had been knocked lopsided, and her forehead was crinkled up in a frown.

"Abi! Thank goodness you're here," Mel said, sounding relieved. "I really need your help."

Chapter Two

"What happened?" Abi stepped into the room, treading carefully through the mess of clothes to reach Mel. Emily followed behind, as Lulu wandered off to explore a pile of doggy accessories.

"I lost the matching hat for one of the fashion show outfits," Mel explained, "and I had to pull out *everything* to find it. Now I need to get this place tidied up, and sort all the clothes and accessories for the fashion show into the right order on the rails, ready to load into the van."

Emily looked around at the chaos, then turned to Mel. "Where do you want us to start?"

Abi smiled. "Mel, this is my very best friend, Emily. Aunt Tiffany said we should help you today." Emily had had plenty of practice helping Abi tidy her room, on days when Abi's mum said she couldn't go out and play until it was spotless. Emily would be a great help today, even if she didn't know how to dress a dog yet!

"Um…" Mel stared at the list in her hand, then at the mess.

"Abi," Emily said, "you know where things are supposed to go around here, right? So if you start by putting things away that we don't need for the show, I can help Mel get the outfits on the rails. Does that sound OK?"

Mel smiled for the first time since they'd arrived. "That would be wonderful. Thank you, Emily."

Working together, they had the wardrobe room back to normal in no time. When Kim the receptionist stuck her head round the door to tell them that the van had arrived to take the outfits over to the hotel, they were ready. Each outfit hung neatly on the wheeled metal rails they were using for the show, complete with a label saying which dog it was for and when they'd be needed on the catwalk. Any accessories were in a see-through bag attached to the hanger, so that they couldn't get lost or muddled up.

The very last outfit on the rail was zipped up in a dark cover, with a "Top Secret" label on it.

Abi nudged Emily. "I wonder what's in there…"

Emily shrugged. "I guess we'll find out later. Come on!"

"Time to go, Lulu!" Abi called, as they prepared to wheel the rails out to the van. Lulu bounced over at the sound of her name.

"What's that in your mouth?" Kneeling down, Abi held out her hand. The little dog dropped a red beret, just the right size for a young bichon frise. Abi fixed it on to Lulu's head.

"It looks perfect," Mel said. "She should keep it on. She wouldn't look out of place on the catwalk!"

Once the rails of doggy outfits were loaded into the van, Mel, Emily, Abi and Lulu piled into the back of a taxi to drive over to the hotel.

"What will you need us to do once we're there, Mel?" Abi asked, as they drove through the London streets.

Lulu sat snuggled up on Emily's lap and rested her paws on Abi's knee.

"Well, first we have to meet with the designer, Nina Grace," Mel said.

Emily's head jerked round to stare at Mel. "*The* Nina Grace?" she asked.

Mel grinned. "That's the one."

"I've never heard of Nina Grace," Abi said, with a frown. "Who is she?"

"She's the best fashion designer in the country! My mum has magazines full of her designs," Emily explained.

"That's right," Mel said. "She's very popular

at the moment. She's designed all the outfits for our human models and worked with me on the doggy ones. We've had meetings with Mrs Travers, who runs the charity, every month for the last year to look at designs and ideas, and narrow down our choices. Nina Grace is a real dog lover – that's why she agreed to help out. We were very lucky to get her."

"It's the Best Friends for Life charity, right?" Abi said. She knew a lot more about animal charities than she did about fashion designers. "They find forever homes for abandoned dogs," she explained to Emily.

"And are those the dogs that are going to be in the fashion show?" Emily asked.

"One or two of them," Mel said. "But mostly they're pedigree dogs and their owners. Mrs Travers held an open audition for models – there were hundreds of people who wanted to be in the show! Mrs Travers and Nina picked the best twenty pairs. In fact," she added, "I think I can see some of them arriving right now…"

Chapter Three

The taxi pulled to a stop in front of a huge white building with men in navy and gold uniforms standing outside. Abi and Emily crammed themselves up against the window to look out, while Mel paid the taxi driver. There were people with suitcases and bags everywhere, all with dogs pulling at their leads to try and get inside. Abi spotted a fireman in uniform with a big Dalmatian, and twins with identical chocolate Labradors.

"Wow," Emily said. "That's a lot of people."

"And a lot of dogs," Abi agreed. The girls were going to have their work cut out getting all the dogs in and out of their outfits.

"Come on," Mel said, opening the taxi door. "Let's go and see if our rails have been unloaded yet."

Inside, the hotel sparkled – there were marble floors and columns and enormous vases filled with flowers. Lulu's claws skittered against the polished floor and Abi's trainers gave a little squeak as she walked. There were more men in navy and gold uniforms, and dotted around the foyer were huge cream sofas and polished low wooden tables.

Mel led the girls past the crowds and straight to a special desk with a banner reading "Best Friends for Life!" above it. At the desk sat an older woman, with short grey hair and a bright purple jacket on. She had a clipboard just like Mel's and on the desk were folders, each with two names and a photo of a dog and their owner.

"Mel! You're here," the woman cried when she spotted them. "Fantastic! And these must be your assistants for the day."

"Hello, Mrs Travers," Mel said, cheerily. "Yes, this is Abi, and this is Emily. And this little beauty investigating your table legs is Lulu."

Mrs Travers smiled and bent down to pet Lulu. "What a beautiful hat, Lulu! The Pooch Parlour van just arrived," she said, straightening up again. "Your rails are being unloaded directly to the doggy dressing room. Nina's already in the ballroom, I think, getting ready to talk to everyone. Most people are here already."

"Great," Mel said. "We'll head over there too, then start getting things ready."

"Hold on. Abi, can you pick up Lulu for a moment?" Mrs Travers whipped out a camera from her bag, and took a quick snap of them all. Then she plugged the camera directly into a mini printer on the desk and printed out the photo. She stuck it to the front of a blank folder, which she handed to Mel. "Inside this folder is everything you need to know about the day. Timetables, maps, names, running orders, phone numbers, everything. So don't lose it!"

"We won't," they promised.

"Mel, you remember where everything is? Good. Well, off you go then." Mrs Travers pointed towards the corridor behind her. "Lots to do!"

Putting Lulu down again, but holding on to her lead, Abi trotted after Mel and Emily as they headed into the hotel. It was time to meet the world-famous designer, Nina Grace!

Abi was glad that their folder had a map in it, and that Mel knew where she was going. The hotel corridors all looked the same and she was sure she'd be lost in no time if she was on her own. Lulu kept trying to stop and sniff around the potted plants and investigate the doors, but Abi kept her close at heel. She didn't want them to fall behind!

Eventually, they came to a set of double doors with a large gold sign that read "Ballroom". Emily glanced nervously at Abi as Mel opened the door. Abi tried to give her friend a reassuring smile, but the truth was, she didn't really know what to expect behind the door either. The Pawchester Hotel was even swankier than Pooch Parlour!

Abi and Emily linked arms, stepped inside the ballroom and looked around. "This is incredible," Emily said.

Abi could only nod. The huge room – bigger by far than her school hall – had been set out with rows and rows of plush chairs for the audience. Then, right at the front and jutting out into the middle of the room, was the catwalk platform. At the back hung a navy velvet curtain, studded with sparkly gems that glittered in the lights.

The room hummed with activity. Dogs jumped up on to the seats and barked for treats from their owners. Grown-ups and children stood around chatting.

They're all waiting to be told what to do next, Abi realized. *Just like us.*

At that moment, the sparkly curtain parted and a woman stepped out on to the catwalk. Dressed in a red knitted dress and a long gold necklace that hung to her waist, she stamped her high-heeled boot against the platform and waited for the room to fall silent.

"Hello, everyone," she said, her voice soft and sweet. "I'm Nina Grace, your designer for the show. I can't wait to get started. How about you?"

Abi stared up at Nina Grace, taking in every word. The designer talked about her own dog, Blue, who had come from a rescue centre, and how he was her inspiration for the show. Then she told them how much money they hoped to raise for the charity that evening.

"Enough to look after every dog at the centre until their perfect forever home can be found!" Nina said, and everyone clapped.

"But now to the show itself. My assistants, Natalie and Sarah, will be backstage to help get you in and out of the designs, and we've brought our own hair stylists and make-up artists too. But the show's not just about you, of course. It's about your gorgeous dogs! So I'm delighted to tell you that the wonderful team from Pooch Parlour will be here to groom and prepare your pets for the catwalk. Please welcome our doggy designer, Mel – where are you, Mel?"

Mel waved, blushing a little as everyone turned to stare at her. "And these are *my* assistants, Abi and Emily." Lulu gave a bark. She didn't want to be forgotten! "And Lulu, of course," Mel added, and everyone laughed.

"Mel and I have worked together to come up with all the adorable outfits your dogs will be wearing in the show. She and the girls will also be backstage to get your dogs in and out of their outfits. Now, if everyone's ready, I'll take you through the curtain to see where the magic is going to happen!"

Chapter Four

Backstage, everything was set up for the dress rehearsal. Beyond the quick-change area just behind the curtain, one large room had been turned into a ladies' dressing room and another was set up for the men. Each had mirrors and dressing tables, with baskets full of hair products and make-up. Nina introduced the models to the hair stylists and make-up artists who would be helping to get them ready.

Emily stared longingly at the other side of the room, where rails full of Nina Grace's designs were lined up against the wall, all carefully labelled with the name of the model and their order in the show, just like the doggy ones had been. One, in a black cover, had a big yellow "Top Secret" sticker on it, the same as the one on the dog costume rail.

Abi could see that Emily really wanted to know what was in there! But Nina was already asking them to move through to the next room – the room that Abi was most interested in. This room, larger than both of the other dressing rooms, had been set up as a mobile Pooch Parlour!

"Hello, everyone," Aunt Tiffany said as the crowd of models and dogs entered. "Welcome to the doggy dressing room!"

Aunt Tiffany had set up mobile grooming stations along one side of the room, each with a Pooch Parlour staff member standing by to primp and pamper the dogs. In the corner was a mini Doggy Daycare to keep the dogs entertained while their owners were busy getting ready. On the other side were the rails of doggy costumes that Abi and Emily had helped Mel prepare. Soon they would get to meet the dogs who were going to wear them!

"Why don't you all take twenty minutes to settle in and learn where everything is," Nina said. "Then we'll start going through the running order and getting you all ready for the dress rehearsal!"

Abi and Emily followed Mel over to the rails to check the dog costumes, while the models milled around. Some headed back to the dressing rooms and others brought their pets over to meet the Pooch Parlour staff and have a look around the grooming stations. Once the models went to their dressing rooms to get ready, the Pooch Parlour staff would be in charge of all the dogs.

Most of the dogs were very well behaved, Abi noticed. That must have been one of the reasons they were picked for the show. With so many different breeds and people backstage, it was important they all got along.

But then she heard a growl, and another one, and a dog started barking wildly. Turning around, Abi saw the twin boys she'd spotted earlier with their Labrador puppies, and a red-haired girl with another dog on a lead. A small, squat, short-haired dog that just wouldn't stop barking!

"Boomer! Quiet." The redheaded girl spoke firmly, and the barking stopped. "Now sit." The dog whimpered a little, but lowered his hindquarters to the floor. "Good boy."

The girl bent down to reward her pet with a treat and a cuddle. "I'm glad I've got you with me today, Boomer."

The boys and their puppies had scampered away across the room by now, and Abi went over to the girl and her dog.

"He's very well trained," Abi said, kneeling down and holding out a hand for him to sniff. "Can I pet him?"

The girl nodded. "His name is Boomer," she said. "And I'm Rachel."

"Hi, Rachel. Hello, Boomer." Abi ran a hand over the little dog's soft coat, and stared at the wrinkles and folds on his face. He was about the same size as Lulu, maybe a little smaller, but otherwise the two dogs were completely different!

"What sort of dog is he?" Emily asked, kneeling beside Abi. Emily was holding Lulu by her lead and the little bichon frise stayed close to the girls. She didn't like a lot of barking – unless she was the one doing it!

"He's a pug," Abi said. She looked up at Rachel. "Right?"

Rachel nodded. "Yep! You can tell by the wrinkles."

"They're kind of weird," Emily said. Cautiously, she reached out with a finger to stroke Boomer's face. "But soft! Hello, Boomer." The dog pressed up against her hand.

"He's very friendly, really," Rachel said. "Those boys were just teasing him. They took the toy he was playing with, so he got a little territorial."

Abi looked over to where the twins were holding out a chew toy for their puppies, then pulling it away again. They all seemed to be enjoying the game, but Abi knew that some dogs didn't like that kind of teasing.

"I just hope Auntie Nina didn't hear him barking," Rachel went on, sounding nervous.

"Auntie Nina?" Emily asked. "Nina Grace is your aunt?"

Rachel nodded, and Emily turned to Abi with a grin. "Sorry, Abi, but that's even cooler than your aunt Tiffany  owning a dog-grooming salon."

Abi laughed. She'd still prefer Pooch Parlour to a clothes shop any day. "Is that how you and Boomer got to be in the show?" Abi asked.

"We auditioned along with everyone else," Rachel told her. "Apparently it was a close thing, but they wanted a pug in the show – they're very popular, you know – and Boomer was the cutest. But I had to promise Auntie Nina that I'd keep him close and wouldn't let him start barking at everyone."

"Does he do that a lot?" Emily asked. "I mean … he was kind of loud."

Abi gave her friend a sympathetic look. Emily liked dogs, but she hadn't spent much time around them and sometimes the louder ones made her uncomfortable.

"He used to," Rachel admitted. "He barked at *everything*. Squirrels in the park, other dogs, strange people, and every single time the phone rang – it drove Mum and Dad up the wall."

"What did you do?" Emily's eyes were wide as she asked the question, as if she couldn't imagine one small dog making so much noise.

Abi smiled to herself. Wait until her friend helped out with bath time at Pooch Parlour – some of the dogs went wild in the water!

"Dad made me take Boomer to a training class," Rachel said. "They taught me how to speak to him to make him pay attention – firmly but calmly. And they helped me train him out of barking all the time. Now it's just sometimes, and I know how to stop him." She glared across at the twins. "Unless someone provokes him."

"That's good," Abi said. "I've done some training with Lulu – it takes ages!"

Lulu lifted her fuzzy head at the sound of her name, red hat still in place, and Rachel beamed. "She's gorgeous! Look, Boomer, a new friend for you."

Abi watched as Lulu cautiously approached the pug. Lulu was a very sociable dog and it was always fun to watch her making new friends. Boomer shuffled back a little, but let Lulu sniff around.

Rachel pulled out some more toys from the basket Aunt Tiffany had set up in the temporary

Doggy Daycare and placed them in front of the dogs. Soon they'd picked one each and were chewing on them happily.

"I bet you're excited about being in the show," Emily said to Rachel.

Abi had a feeling that her friend would rather be on the catwalk than helping with the dogs backstage.

"Yes! But scared too," Rachel said. "I'm so nervous my tummy feels funny, and I'm hot all over."

"I bet you'll feel better after the dress rehearsal," Abi said. "It always helps me when I know exactly what's going to be happening." She'd feel a lot better about everything herself, she thought, once she and Emily had had a chance to practise dressing the dogs in their costumes.

"I hope so. What are you two going to be doing in the show?" Rachel asked. "I don't remember seeing either of you at the auditions."

"Oh, we're not models," Abi said cheerfully. "We're here to help get the dogs in and out of their costumes."

"Wow! That sounds fun," Rachel said. "I can't wait to see what all the outfits look like."

"Me neither," Emily said.

"Well, there's not long to wait now," Abi said. "Look, here's Nina. The dress rehearsal must be about to start!"

Chapter Five

As Nina Grace and her assistants began organizing all of the models in the dressing rooms, Aunt Tiffany and her team took charge of the dogs.

Abi helped Rachel get Boomer settled and listened as the groomer explained how they would clean the folds and wrinkles of the pug's face using cotton buds. Then Abi waved goodbye to Rachel as she went off to get changed, and headed back over to where Mel was sorting through the rails of outfits.

"What do we need to do, Mel?" Abi asked, as Lulu trotted over to her. Emily had taken Lulu off her lead, now that things had calmed down a bit.

"We need to teach you girls to dress the dogs," Mel replied.

"Um, about that," Emily said, as Mel started sorting through the outfits. "How *do* you put clothes on a dog?"

Mel laughed. "Pretty much the same way you dress a child. Have either of you ever helped change a baby or toddler? No? Well, never mind! Come on, I'll show you. Abi, do you want to see if you can find a few spare outfits that might fit Lulu, so that you can both have a trial go? I'll see if Tiffany can lend us one of the other dogs for a little while, so you can get a feel for dressing bigger animals too."

"Have you done this before?" Emily asked Abi.

Abi shrugged. "A bit. Lulu never really wore clothes until we came to Pooch Parlour this summer, but since then we've had masses of fun trying on outfits." She frowned. "Maybe it's a bit different when you're trying to dress dogs you don't know very well, though."

"Especially if you've never done it before," Emily said, nervously.

"You'll be fine," Abi reassured her. She flicked through the hangers on the rail, looking for things that might fit Lulu. "Besides, that's what the dress rehearsal is for – so we can practise and get used to the dogs, and for the dogs and models to learn what they have to do."

"Exactly right, Abi," Mel said, returning with the beautiful Dalmatian Abi had spotted earlier. "For most of the dogs, this will be their first time in a fashion show and I'm sure they're all just as nervous as we are."

"You're nervous too?" Emily asked Mel, although she sounded like she didn't believe it.

Mel laughed. "Of course I am! This is a big night for all of us, and everyone wants it to go smoothly, so we can raise lots of money for the homeless dogs. That's why we're having a dress rehearsal – so we can feel confident tonight about what we need to do."

"That makes sense," Emily said, looking a little happier.

"Good!" Abi said. "We'd better get practising, then."

"OK," Mel said. "We'll start with Lulu, since she knows us all. Then we'll move on to Hero," she added, stroking a hand over the Dalmatian's coat.

Abi called Lulu, and she came scampering over, a chew toy in her mouth. She stayed close to Abi when she spotted Hero, but the bigger dog lowered his nose to sniff at Lulu, and soon the little bichon frise was sniffing back.

"I wonder why's he called Hero," Emily said, watching the two dogs getting to know each other.

"He's a fire station dog, I think," Abi said. "I saw him with a man in a firefighter's uniform earlier."

Mel nodded. "That's right. Lots of fire stations used to have Dalmatians as mascots." She grinned at the two dogs as Lulu placed the chew toy down in front of Hero, happy to share with her new friend. "And now we've all got to know one another, we should get to work! Abi, which outfits did you find for Lulu?"

Abi held out the three outfits she'd chosen, all designed for some of the smaller dogs in the show. They wouldn't be a perfect fit, but they'd be close enough for practising.

"Great!" Mel took two and passed one to Emily. "OK. I'll put Lulu in this outfit first, so you can both watch how I do it. Then Abi can take the outfit off and put the next one on. Then Emily can do the same."

Abi was sure that Lulu would love the chance to try on so many outfits! "OK," she said, and Emily nodded.

"Lulu! Come, Lulu," Mel called, and the fluffy dog padded over. "Let's get you into this pretty outfit."

Abi watched carefully as Mel removed the red beret and eased Lulu's head through the neck of the jumper, then lifted each front leg in turn to pull it through. Next, she smoothed the jumper down over Lulu's springy coat, and finally added a matching hat to her head.

"See?" Mel said. "Easy. Abi, your turn."

Abi took a breath. She wanted to get this exactly right. After all, if she couldn't dress her own dog, what chance did she have with a dozen strange animals?

Carefully, she removed the hat and handed it back to Mel. Then she took the jumper off again by doing the exact reverse of what she'd watched Mel do.

"First the legs," she muttered to herself, lifting Lulu's left paw, then her right, to slip them out of the sleeves. Lulu gave a friendly little bark, as if to say, *This is fun!* "Good girl, Lulu. You like all this fuss, don't you?" Abi tugged the jumper over her head. "And I promise you can have some treats when we're finished."

Jumper off, Abi turned to the second outfit, confident that she had the hang of it now. Except the next outfit wasn't the same at all.

When she'd chosen it from the rack, still in its hanging case, she'd thought it looked like a dress.

But instead it was a navy blue jacket with a tie, just like Dad wore when he had an important meeting at work. Abi blinked at it for a moment, trying to figure out how on earth to put it on Lulu.

Then she spotted the Velcro fastener at the collar. She pulled it open, and placed it around Lulu's neck before closing it again. She repeated the steps with Lulu's legs, lifting each paw to put into the coat. Finally, she fastened the last closure under her belly.

"That's great, Abi!" Mel moved closer, and held up a small elasticated loop at the back of the coat. "Where do you think this goes?"

"Under her tail?" Abi guessed.

"That's right!" Mel said.

Abi tucked the loop under Lulu's tail then sat back to admire her handiwork. Lulu looked very smart indeed in the coat. Maybe she'd talk to her mum about getting Lulu one of her own, she thought. A pink one, perhaps…

"Right, Emily," Mel said. "Your turn. Do you know what to do now?"

"I think so," Emily said.

Abi watched her take a deep breath and she silently cheered her friend on. Emily could do it, Abi knew she could!

But before Emily could even start to take off Lulu's coat, there was a sudden scream from the dressing rooms…

Chapter Six

Abi, Mel and Emily all looked at each other, then quickly got to their feet. Barking, Hero ran for the door, and they all followed, Lulu scampering behind them in her lovely blue jacket.

A crowd had already formed at the door to the girls' dressing room but they let Mel through, and Emily and Abi slipped in behind her, Lulu weaving her way through all the legs. Abi hadn't had time to put Lulu back on her lead in the rush to find out what was going on.

"What's happened?" Mel asked, eyes wide with alarm.

One of the make-up artists looked up, her face pale. "Oh, I'm sorry for scaring everyone. It's just… Look!"

She pointed, and the girl having her make-up done spun her chair around so she was facing them. Abi gasped! It was Rachel – and her face was covered in red spots!

Rachel stared back at the crowd miserably while the make-up artist chattered on. "She was fine when she sat down, I swear! Then all of a sudden these
spots started appearing, one after another.

A new spot, every few seconds. Do you think it's my make-up? I've never had a problem before, I promise."

Mel shook her head. "I don't think it's your make-up," she said. "I'm afraid it's much worse than that. I think it's chickenpox."

Abi peered closer at the spots on Rachel's face. They did look a lot like the ones she and Emily had had when they were five. There was still a photo on Abi's bedroom wall of the two of them together – they had both caught chickenpox at the exact same time. Mum said that's when she knew they'd be friends for life.

"I'll call the doctor," Mel said. "Can someone find Nina? She's your aunt, right?" she asked Rachel, who nodded. "She can call your parents."

"But what about the show?" one of the twins asked from the doorway.

"Yeah, we want to be on the stage," the other said.

"And you will be." Nina Grace appeared at just the right time. "We'll make sure Rachel is well looked after, but the show must go on! Someone else will have to wear Rachel's outfits and lead Boomer out on to the catwalk. After all, he's wearing the secret showstopper outfit in the finale! We can't do it without him."

Abi and Emily exchanged a glance at the words "secret showstopper".

"First," Mel said, looking around the room, "is there anyone here who hasn't had chickenpox before? If you've already had it, you should be fine."

Emily nodded. "That's right. My mum is a doctor and she says it's very rare to catch chickenpox more than once."

"Just as well we had it when we were five, then," Abi said, nudging her friend.

Emily rolled her eyes. "That was so unfair. I was covered in spots and you only had about five!"

Abi laughed. "Just lucky, I guess!" She watched as Nina led Rachel out to another room to wait for her mum. Rachel looked anything *but* lucky. "Poor Rachel."

"Yeah. She said earlier she was feeling almost sick with nerves," Emily replied.

"Guess it wasn't nerves, after all."

"She was so close to being in a real fashion show. How awful to have to go home at the last moment," Emily said. "I wonder who they'll get to replace her."

Abi looked around. There weren't any other girl models of Rachel's age, as far as she could see. In fact, the closest girl was … Emily! Abi smiled a secret smile. Maybe her friend's dream would come true after all!

"Right then," Nina said, coming back into the room. "What's next?"

"It looks like everyone else has already had chickenpox," Mel told her. "So at least we don't need to worry about anyone looking spottier than Hero on the catwalk."

Everyone laughed, and Hero gave a sharp bark at the sound.

"So now we just need a replacement model for Rachel," Nina said, gazing around the room.

She stopped, looking at Abi and Emily. "Mel, I'm sure you don't really need two assistants, do you?"

"What do you think, girls?" Mel asked. "Fancy trying out as models instead of dog dressers?"

Abi saw the excitement on Emily's face, the way her friend clasped her hands tightly together. It would be fun to be out on the catwalk, but…

"Emily should do it," Abi said. "She's closer to Rachel's height, and I know the dogs better so I'll be more useful backstage."

"She has a point," Mel agreed, but Nina just narrowed her eyes at Abi.

"I think you should both try out," Nina said, finally. "You can each take one of Rachel's outfits for the dress rehearsal, and when you're not on the catwalk you can help Mel with the

dogs. Then whichever one of you is best can put on the showstopper outfit for the finale and take part in the show tonight. OK?"

The secret outfit! Abi hoped that they'd get a sneak preview.

"OK!" Emily said, grinning.

Abi nodded, feeling a little bit pleased. At least she could try on one of the outfits and see how it felt to be on a real catwalk, even if she didn't get to be in the show!

"In that case, time to get to work! Dress rehearsal starts in fifteen minutes, everyone!" Nina clapped her hands, and everyone scurried off to where they were supposed to be, the dressing rooms buzzing with activity again.

Chapter Seven

Emily went first. Abi watched as her friend was whisked off to have her hair and make-up done. But Mel still had plenty of work to keep Abi busy! First, she practised getting Hero in and out of his outfits. It was trickier with a dog she didn't know as well as Lulu – and especially one with much longer legs! But she managed and Hero was very well behaved.

"Good boy," Abi told Hero, giving him a treat.

The big dog wolfed it down in a moment.

"Your turn," Emily said cheerfully from behind her.

Abi turned to look at her friend. Emily looked very grown up with her hair pinned back and lipstick on. Abi's mum was very strict about make-up, although she knew that Emily got to try on her mum's sometimes.

"Wow!" Abi said, grinning. "I like your hair! Was it fun having it done?"

"Lots," Emily said, dropping down to sit next to Hero. She hadn't put on her fashion-show outfit yet, because Nina didn't want her to get dog hairs all over it. She'd get changed just before it was time to go on. "Go and find out – they're waiting for you. And I want to see what you look like with make-up on! Besides, I need to practise dressing Lulu and Hero."

Abi didn't think Emily would need to know how to dress the dogs. She'd be up on the catwalk! Still, Emily did love dogs and it would be fun if they both knew how to dress Lulu in the future.

In the dressing room, the air was heavy with hairspray and perfume. Abi sat in the chair and let the hair stylist get to work, while she watched everything that was going on in the mirror.

"I'm not Harry," one of the twins said, as Nina's assistant, Sarah, held out his first outfit. "I'm Henry."

"Oh!" Sarah pulled the outfit back and reached for the next one. "I'm sorry." She handed him the correct outfit, then turned to the other twin with his.

"I'm not Harry!" the second twin said. "Don't listen to him. *I'm* Henry."

"Well, you can't both be Henry!" Sarah snapped, swapping the costumes again as the boys fell about laughing. "And we don't have time for these sort of games today."

Sarah stalked off to give someone else their costumes, but the boys were still laughing. Somehow Abi didn't think they'd get bored of this game any time soon. Normally, she'd think it was a bit funny, but not today, when everyone

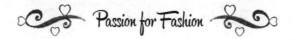

was working so hard to make the show perfect.

"Right," the hair stylist said to Abi. "That's your hair done. Now Jenny is going to do your make-up!" Abi looked at her reflection. She hardly recognized herself!

Jenny spun the chair around to face her, ready to put on Abi's make-up. "Close your eyes, please."

"I bet you they can't tell our dogs apart either," she heard Henry – or was it Harry? – say. Well, that was just where they were wrong, Abi thought. Telling dogs apart was easy compared to identical twins!

"How's it going?" Abi asked, as she arrived back at the dog's costume station, and found Lulu half in, half out of a pink dress with a frilly, sequinned skirt.

"Really well," Mel said, enthusiastically. "Emily's definitely getting the hang of it now."

"It's fun," Emily agreed, easing Lulu's leg through a sleeve, then looking up at her friend. "Abi, I love your hair!"

"You look gorgeous," Mel said. "And I think we're just about prepared for the dress rehearsal now. Which is lucky because here come the first dogs, ready for their outfits!"

The Pooch Parlour staff brought the dogs over on their leads, one by one. First up was Hero, who already knew them, and stood very patiently as Abi dressed him in his waistcoat with tiny white spots on black satin, to mirror his natural coat. Emily fastened the bow-tie collar around his neck, then led him back to his owner, who wore a very smart suit with a matching waistcoat.

"See?" Emily said. "This is going to be easy."

But then Abi saw who the Pooch Parlour groomers were bringing over next – the chocolate Labs. And the twins were approaching too, ready to take their dogs. "Watch out for these two," she whispered to Emily, but her friend just looked confused.

Abi stared at the boys as they approached. They truly were identical, although their outfits were different. Their dogs' outfits were matched to theirs, so it was important to get them the right way round. But from what she'd heard earlier, she suspected that the twins would try to swap their outfits, just to confuse everyone!

"You can't tell us apart, can you?" The twin who'd spoken flashed his brother a look.

"Don't worry," his brother said. "Almost no one can. Even our mum gets confused sometimes."

"I'm Harry, and this is Freddie," the first twin

said, patting his Labrador puppy on the head.

"And I'm Henry, and this is Frankie," said the other twin, pointing to his own puppy.

Abi studied them carefully. Each puppy seemed very devoted to their own twin, so she was pretty sure they wouldn't just swap dogs. Looking at the labels on the costume bags, she realized that the names didn't match up, though.

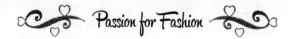

Frankie's costume matched Henry's outfit, and Freddie's costume matched Harry's! But which was the wrong way round? The boys' costumes or the dogs' names?

Chapter Eight

Emily was staring at the costumes and then the boys in confusion. "Hang on," she said. "If that's Frankie…" As she said the name, the dog the twins had told them was Freddie looked up.

Abi grinned. That was it! The dogs knew their real names, even if the boys mixed them up. "Freddie!" she called, and the dog standing with Henry ran forward to her.

Nina suddenly appeared behind them. "Looks like the dogs can tell themselves apart better than you can, boys. At least I know *their* costumes will be the right way round. You two will just have to make sure that yours match up now, won't you?"

"Yes, Miss Grace," the boys said, looking sullen.

Abi didn't care if the boys were cross about having their fun ruined. The most important thing was making the show a success!

"And, Emily," Nina added, watching as Abi's friend slipped Frankie into his waistcoat. "You'd better go and get changed, if you're going on with Boomer."

"And I'd better help get Boomer into his costume," Abi agreed, spotting the pug being led over from Aunt Tiffany's grooming table.

Abi was kept very busy getting all the dogs into their costumes, but Mel told her to take a break when it was Emily's turn on the catwalk, so she slipped over to the edge of the curtain to wish her friend luck.

Each of the models had to queue up in order beside the curtain, as soon as they were ready in their costumes. Nina's assistant, Natalie, stood there with a clipboard, telling people when it was time to go out, and ticking off each model as they went. So far, it was all going smoothly.

"You'll be great out there," Abi said, handing Emily Boomer's lead. Emily wore a beautiful lacy dress that came down to her knees, and a fluffy white cardigan over the top. Boomer had a red and white waistcoat on, and a matching bowler hat! "Are you ready?"

"I think so," Emily said, but her voice shook as she spoke.

"You're on!" whispered Natalie, and gave Emily a gentle push to get her to move through the curtain.

Abi held her breath as her friend walked out on to the catwalk. She could see Emily's legs

wobbling just a little, but she kept her head up high and walked straight.

She'll be fine, Abi thought.

But then she looked at Boomer.

The little pug was pulling on his lead, straining towards the twins and their dogs, as they walked back towards the curtain.

"Oh no…" Abi whispered, but there was nothing she could do, no way to warn Emily what was about to happen.

"Boomer!" Emily cried, as the pug dragged her across the catwalk, barking wildly.

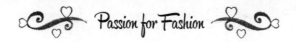

"Oi! Get away from Freddie!" Henry yelled back, yanking on his puppy's lead to try and keep him away.

But it was no good. Boomer jumped up at Henry, and Harry dashed over to try to stop him. But Boomer kept jumping and barking, and Abi could see that Emily was barely keeping hold of Boomer's lead. Nina approached the catwalk, probably to try and stop the rehearsal. Emily would never be allowed to take Boomer out for the show if that happened!

Abi had to help. Slipping through the curtain before Natalie could stop her, she tried to remember exactly how Rachel had controlled Boomer earlier that day.

Calm but firm, she told herself. *That's the key.*

"Boomer," Abi said, careful not to shout, but loud enough that the pug couldn't ignore her. "Down, Boomer. Quiet."

Boomer turned away from the boys and their puppies to look at Abi. He gave one last bark, then stopped.

"Good boy," Abi said, motioning for the twins to get off the catwalk. She fished in her pocket for a treat to give Boomer. "He'll be fine now, Emily," she assured her friend. But Emily was shaking worse than ever. "Go on, you can do it," Abi said.

Emily shook her head. "I think you'd better be the model for tonight's show, Abi," she said. "Boomer needs you holding his lead."

"Are you sure?" Abi asked. She knew how much Emily had wanted to be in the fashion show.

"Very." Emily gave a wobbly laugh. "I'll be much happier backstage with Mel, trust me!"

"OK then." Abi took Boomer's lead, and walked to the end of the catwalk with him, trying to imagine that she was wearing the same fancy outfit as Emily.

At the end of the catwalk she paused and smiled out into the imaginary audience, Boomer waiting patiently at heel.

"That's great, Abi," Nina said, from the front row. "Just wait there for a moment, let everyone see the outfit, then turn and walk slowly back."

Abi did as she was told, feeling a little nervous as she headed back towards the curtain and spotted the next model walking towards them. Keeping a tight grip on Boomer's lead, she tried to stay calm as he pulled ahead a little, towards the approaching dog.

"Quiet, Boomer," Abi said when Boomer barked, just once. She hoped Nina couldn't hear. But Boomer pulled back and stayed at her side, silent now. Abi let out a huge sigh of relief as she made it back through the curtains.

Chapter Nine

"You did it!" Emily whooped, wrapping her arms around Abi. "You were brilliant!"

"Shh!" Natalie hissed, and Abi and Emily skipped down towards the doggy dressing room.

"Boomer did it," Abi said.

"Because you knew how to control him." Emily sighed. "Maybe I'll wait until I can star in an ordinary fashion show. One without dogs."

"You're sure you don't mind me being the model for the show?" Abi asked. As fun as it was, she didn't want to do it if it would upset her friend.

"I'm sure," Emily said, firmly. "I had great fun having my hair and make-up done and trying on the dress. But you're much better with Boomer than me. Besides, I'm getting loads of practice dressing the dogs. It's fun. I think I'd like being a doggy designer more than a dog trainer."

Abi smiled. For Abi, getting to know new dogs and teaching them how to behave was best of all.

"Abi, you'd better get into Rachel's next outfit," Mel said. "You'll be on again soon."

"I'll dress Boomer," Emily said, then glared at the little pug. "As long as he promises not to bark at me this time."

"Have fun," Abi said, and skipped off to the dressing room to find Sarah, and her outfit.

The rest of the dress rehearsal went smoothly. Abi and Boomer strutted their stuff on the catwalk twice more. They didn't have to go on straight after the twins again, so it was fairly easy to keep Boomer calm. For the second time, everyone was in their finale costumes – except Abi. Nina wanted to save her surprise outfit for the show itself.

Emily and Mel kept all the dogs in order and in the right costumes, and Abi grinned at them as she collected Boomer. He didn't have his last, top-secret, show-stopping number on either, although Nina promised that it would be a perfect match for Abi's outfit.

"I want to see the secret outfits," Emily complained.

"Not as much as me," Abi said. "I'm the one who has to wear it! I hope it's nice."

"Well, you'll both have to be patient for just

a little bit longer," Mel said, with a mysterious smile. "But I think you'll like it!"

All the models and dogs were onstage together for the grand finale, and as they lined up, Nina, Mel, the assistants, the Pooch Parlour staff, Emily and Lulu all gathered at the front of the catwalk to cheer and clap.

"That was really fantastic, everyone," Nina said, beaming broadly. "I just know tonight is going to be a huge success."

"Now, can you all take your dogs back to the doggy dressing room, then make your way back to your own dressing rooms, please," Sarah said. "We need everyone out of their outfits until it's time for the real show to start, so make sure you hang everything up on the right hanger, and that the label with your name and the running order number is still attached."

Abi turned with the rest of the models, ready to get changed and have a break before the evening show.

"Oh, except you, Abi," Nina called. "We still need to adjust your outfits to make sure they're a perfect fit!"

Abi glanced down at where Mel and Emily stood with Lulu. She'd planned to go and help them get all the dogs out of their costumes and prepare for the evening.

"Don't worry," Emily called. "We'll take care

of Lulu. And the other dogs!"

Abi followed Nina to one of the smaller backstage rooms, where she stood on a stool while the designer pinned and tucked each of the first two outfits in turn, to adjust for the differences between Rachel and Abi. Rachel was a few centimetres taller than she was, and Abi didn't want to trip over the trousers she wore in the second outfit! Even then, Abi didn't get to see the secret finale outfit. They took some measurements to adjust it, and that was that!

Nina sent the clothes off with Sarah and Natalie to be quickly altered and Abi, dressed in her own clothes again, headed back towards the doggy dressing room to help with all the pups.

"Not so fast, missy," one of the stylists called out as she passed. "You'd better get in here. We've still got to touch up your make-up and fix your hair!"

Abi sighed. A model's work was never done!

Chapter Ten

It didn't seem like very much later when Nina stuck her head into the dressing room.

"The audience are all in their seats!" she told the models. "I've got to go out front now and get things started, but I just wanted to wish you all lots of luck. I know you'll be brilliant!"

The room was abuzz with nervous chatter.

Abi smoothed down the lacy dress Emily had worn earlier. It was a perfect fit for Abi now, and the black shoes she wore it with even had a tiny heel. She just hoped Boomer would behave…

"Good luck!" Emily whispered as she handed Abi Boomer's lead. The twins were already out on the catwalk and any moment now it would be her turn.

Kneeling down, she stared into Boomer's eyes. "OK, Boomer," she said, quietly. "This is it. We're going to go out there, do our thing, then walk back again. No barking, no jumping up, nothing. Understand?"

Boomer tilted his head to the side as he stared back at her.

Abi sighed. She'd have to hope for the best.

"You're up," Natalie whispered. "Good luck."

With a deep breath, Abi stepped through the curtain, smile in place, Boomer at her side. Her hands felt sweaty and slippery as they held the lead, and the lights that pointed down at her from above were so bright she could hardly see beyond the front row of the audience. The twins and their puppies were walking towards them, so she kept Boomer's lead very short.

She knew the moment Boomer spotted the twins, because he tugged on the lead.

"Heel, Boomer," Abi said quietly, and Boomer fell back. Moments later, they were past the twins and Abi felt her whole body start to relax. Now she could enjoy the show!

The rest of the evening went past in a blur of changing costumes, having powder dusted over her face and clutching Boomer's lead in her hand, the wrinkly dog panting beside her.

Before she knew it, Abi was stepping out on to the catwalk in her last outfit of the evening – Nina's true masterpiece.

She'd gasped when Nina had finally unzipped the case in the dressing room. Her secret finale outfit was a princess's ball dress!

Abi smoothed down the pale blue satin skirts that fell all the way to the floor from the bodice, and stretched out her arms in their flouncy sleeves. It was beautiful! She even had a little tiara clipped into her hair.

Boomer was dressed as her Prince Charming, in a matching blue frock coat and a little golden crown. He strutted proudly out on to the catwalk in front of her, and the audience gasped then started to clap.

As the cast of models and dogs all lined up along the catwalk, the audience's applause grew louder and they started cheering and stomping. Abi's face hurt from grinning so much, but she couldn't stop. They'd done it! The fashion show had been a success!

Looking down at the edge of the catwalk she saw Aunt Tiffany, Mel and Emily cheering. At Emily's feet, Lulu yapped excitedly, and Abi's best friend was busy taking photos in between cheers.

Mrs Travers climbed the steps from the audience on to the catwalk, and they all shuffled along to make room for her.

"Ladies, gentlemen and dogs," she said, as the audience settled down to listen. "Thank you all so much for coming today. This show would not have been possible without your support – and without the support of everyone who has taken part. From our brilliant designer, Nina Grace…" More clapping, as Nina took a bow. "To the stylists and the staff of Pooch Parlour. A huge thank you to our gorgeous models and their humans, especially Abi, who stepped in at the very last moment to help us out –" Abi blushed, as everyone from Pooch Parlour cheered even louder at her name – "And to everyone here in the audience tonight, I want to say the biggest possible thank you. Finally," Mrs Travers added, shouting over the clapping.

"Finally, I am delighted to tell you that we have totally smashed our fundraising target for the night!"

The whole room exploded into another, even louder round of clapping, whistling, whooping and stomping.

"Thanks to all of you, Best Friends for Life

will be able to look after many, many more dogs, while we find them their forever homes."

Abi clapped and cheered louder than anyone else at this, grinning down at Lulu and Emily. She was so lucky to have her own best friends, and now she'd helped other people – and dogs – to find theirs.

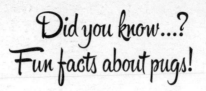

Did you know...?
Fun facts about pugs!

Pugs are one of the oldest breeds of dog.
They were first bred in China almost 2,500 years ago.

A group of pugs is called a grumble.

The famous emperor of France, Napoleon, had a pug
named Fortune. When Napoleon was in prison, his
wife used Fortune to deliver secret messages to him.
She hid them inside his collar!

Unlike most other dogs, pugs aren't very good at
swimming. Their short legs and stocky bodies make
it difficult for them to move in the water.

Pugs spend most of their time sleeping. The average
healthy pug can sleep for almost 14 hours a day!

Look out for the next
Pooch Parlour

Wedding Tails

Out in
Jan 2015

Wedding bells are ringing! The happy couple want
their pet dalmatians to walk down the aisle with the
rings, so Pooch Parlour is on hand for the big day.
The only trouble is getting the playful pups to stay
in one place! Can Abi help them act the part?

Polka and Smudge are in the spotlight!

Read more from
Pooch Parlour

V.I.P.
(Very Important Pup!)

Welcome to Pooch Parlour, where every dog gets star treatment!

Abi is over the moon to be spending the summer at Pooch Parlour, her aunt Tiffany's luxury grooming salon. She can't believe her luck when a famous actress and her adorable Pomeranian Jade appear! Can Abi impress them with the Pooch Parlour pampering treatments?

Jade wants to sparkle!

Pooch Parlour

V.I.P.
(Very Important Pup!)

Katy Cannon

Dog Star

Welcome to Pooch Parlour, where every dog gets star treatment!

When Abi hears that Pooch Parlour will be the official salon for a group of gorgeous dog stars, she is thrilled! She will be grooming the most glamorous dogs in town! But can Abi help a perky little Yorkie called Pickle to get her big break?

Pickle wants to shine!

Pooch Parlour

Dog Star

Katy Cannon

How to be a Pooch-Pampering Professional!

Dog grooming can be heaps of fun for both you and your pup – but it's important to know the right techniques!

Follow our top tips for the perfect pamper:

Make a Splash!

Some pooches love baths, but for others they can be a bit scary. Try giving your pup treats in the tub, so he or she connects water with having fun.

Brush Up!

A dog's coat needs brushing to keep it glossy. Even if your pup is short-haired like Hugo, regular brushing will help to remove loose dead hairs and keep your pooch's fur slick and clean so they look and feel their best.

Perfect Match!

Find out what kind of brush is right
for your breed of dog. A fluff-ball like
Jade needs a pin brush, whereas a curved
wire brush is best for Lulu's wavy fur.
Ask your breeder or local dog-grooming
parlour for advice.

Smooth Moves!

Sometimes a dog's fur can get tangled
into clumps called "mats", though regular
brushing will help prevent this. If your poor
pup's coat is matted, ask an adult to help you
rub some baby oil into the knots before very
gently combing them out with your fingers.

Natural Beauty!

Dogs come in a range of beautiful colours and it's
best to keep it that way! Dyeing a dog's fur can
cause an allergic reaction, making your pup very
uncomfortable. The staff at Pooch Parlour never dye
a dog's fur – the pups are gorgeous just as they are!

Katy Cannon was born in the United Arab Emirates, grew up in North Wales and now lives in Hertfordshire with her husband and daughter Holly.

Katy loves animals, and grew up with a cat, lots of fish and a variety of gerbils. One of her favourite pastimes is going on holiday to the seaside, where she can paddle in the sea and eat fish and chips!

For more about the author, visit her website:

www.katycannon.com

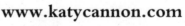